EMMETT

and the Bright Blue Cape

by Alyssa Satin Capucilli ★ illustrated by Henry Cole

Ready-to-Read

Simon Spotlight

New York   London   Toronto   Sydney   New Delhi

For Peter,
who loved to wear his cape . . . everywhere!
—A. S. C.

For Mason
—H. C.

SIMON SPOTLIGHT
An imprint of Simon & Schuster Children's Publishing Division
1230 Avenue of the Americas, New York, New York 10020
This Simon Spotlight edition September 2017
Text copyright © 2017 by Alyssa Satin Capucilli
Illustrations copyright © 2008 and 2017 by Henry Cole
All rights reserved, including the right of reproduction in whole or in part in any form.
SIMON SPOTLIGHT, READY-TO-READ, and colophon are registered trademarks of Simon & Schuster, Inc.
For information about special discounts for bulk purchases, please contact Simon & Schuster Special Sales at
1-866-506-1949 or business@simonandschuster.com.
Manufactured in the United States of America 0817 LAK
10 9 8 7 6 5 4 3 2 1
This book has been cataloged with the Library of Congress.
ISBN 978-1-4814-5869-6 (pbk)
ISBN 978-1-4814-5873-3 (hc)
ISBN 978-1-4814-5874-0 (eBook)

Emmett Duck loved his bright blue cape.

"Quack! Quack! Whee!
Super Emmett can run
faster than the wind."

"He can jump higher
than the sky.
Super Emmett can fly!
Quack! Quack! Whee!"

Emmett wore his cape when
he rode his scooter.

He wore it
to the park.

He wore
it to the
library.

Emmett wore
his cape
everywhere!

"Are you ever going to take
that cape off?"
asked his big sister, Katy.

"Never!" said Emmett.

One morning, Mrs. Duck said,
"The sun is shining, and
the birds are chirping.

Today is the perfect day
to wash your cape."

"Quack! Quack! Hmpfh!"
said Emmett.
"How can I be a superhero
without my cape?"

"Tra-la-la. Quack! Quack!
You can wear my boa,"
said Katy Duck.

"I can only be a superhero with my bright blue cape," Emmett told Katy.

"Well, even superheroes wear **clean** bright blue capes," said Mrs. Duck.

She washed the cape and hung it outside to dry.

But when Emmett went to
get his cape . . . it was gone!

"Quack! Quack! Waaah!
Where is my cape?"

Emmett looked under the swing.

He looked in the shed.

He looked behind the tree.

Then he looked up!

There was a bird.

Tweet! Tweet!

The bird tugged and pulled.

Soon the cape did not look

like a cape anymore.

Instead, it was a nest.

A bright blue nest.

"How can I be a superhero now?" asked Emmett.

"I have an idea,"
said Mrs. Duck.
Emmett snipped and snipped.
Mrs. Duck sewed and sewed.

And then . . .

"Super Emmett can run.

He can jump.

He can fly!"

"Super Emmett can help build a nest too! Quack! Quack! Whee!"

Tweet! Tweet!